STONE ARCH BOOKS
a capstone imprint

THE BATMAN STRIKES! ®

▼▼ STONE ARCH BOOKS™

Published in 2014
A Capstone Imprint
1710 Roe Crest Drive
North Mankato, MN 56003
www.capstonepub.com

Originally published by DC Comics in the U.S. in
single magazine form as The Batman Strikes! #8.
Copyright © 2014 DC Comics. All Rights Reserved.

DC Comics
1700 Broadway, New York, NY 10019
A Warner Bros. Entertainment Company

Printed in China.
032014 008085LEOF14

Cataloging-in-Publication Data is available at the
Library of Congress website:
ISBN: 978-1-4342-9229-2 (library binding)

Summary: Gotham City's never been hotter, which
can only mean one thing: Firefly is back. Batman
must stop this pyromaniac before Gotham is
reduced to ash!

STONE ARCH BOOKS
Ashley C. Andersen Zantop Publisher
Michael Dahl Editorial Director
Sean Tulien Editor
Heather Kindseth Creative Director
Bob Lentz Designer
Tori Abraham Production Specialist

DC COMICS
Joan Hilty & Harvey Richards Original U.S. Editors
Jeff Matsuda & Dave McCaig Cover Artists

THE BATMAN IS ON FIRE!

BILL MATHENY ....WRITER
CHRISTOPHER JONES ....PENCILLER
TERRY BEATTY..INKER
HEROIC AGE..COLORIST
PAT BROSSEAU ....LETTERER

**BATMAN CREATED BY
BOB KANE**

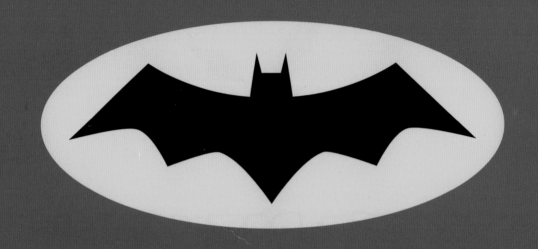

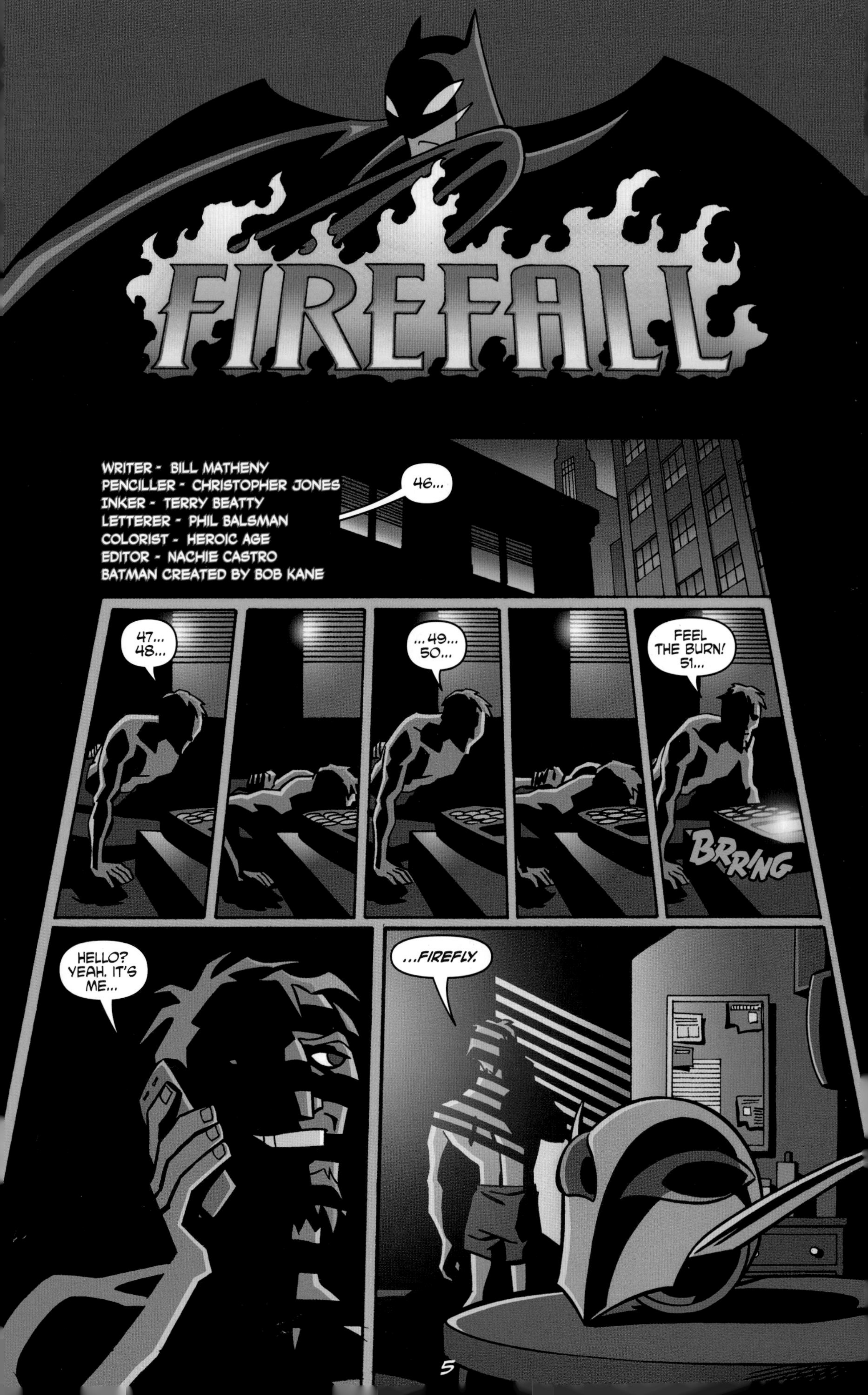
FIREFALL
WRITER - BILL MATHENY
PENCILLER - CHRISTOPHER JONES
INKER - TERRY BEATTY
LETTERER - PHIL BALSMAN
COLORIST - HEROIC AGE
EDITOR - NACHIE CASTRO
BATMAN CREATED BY BOB KANE
46...
47... 48...
...49... 50...
FEEL THE BURN! 51...
BRRING
HELLO? YEAH. IT'S ME...
...FIREFLY.

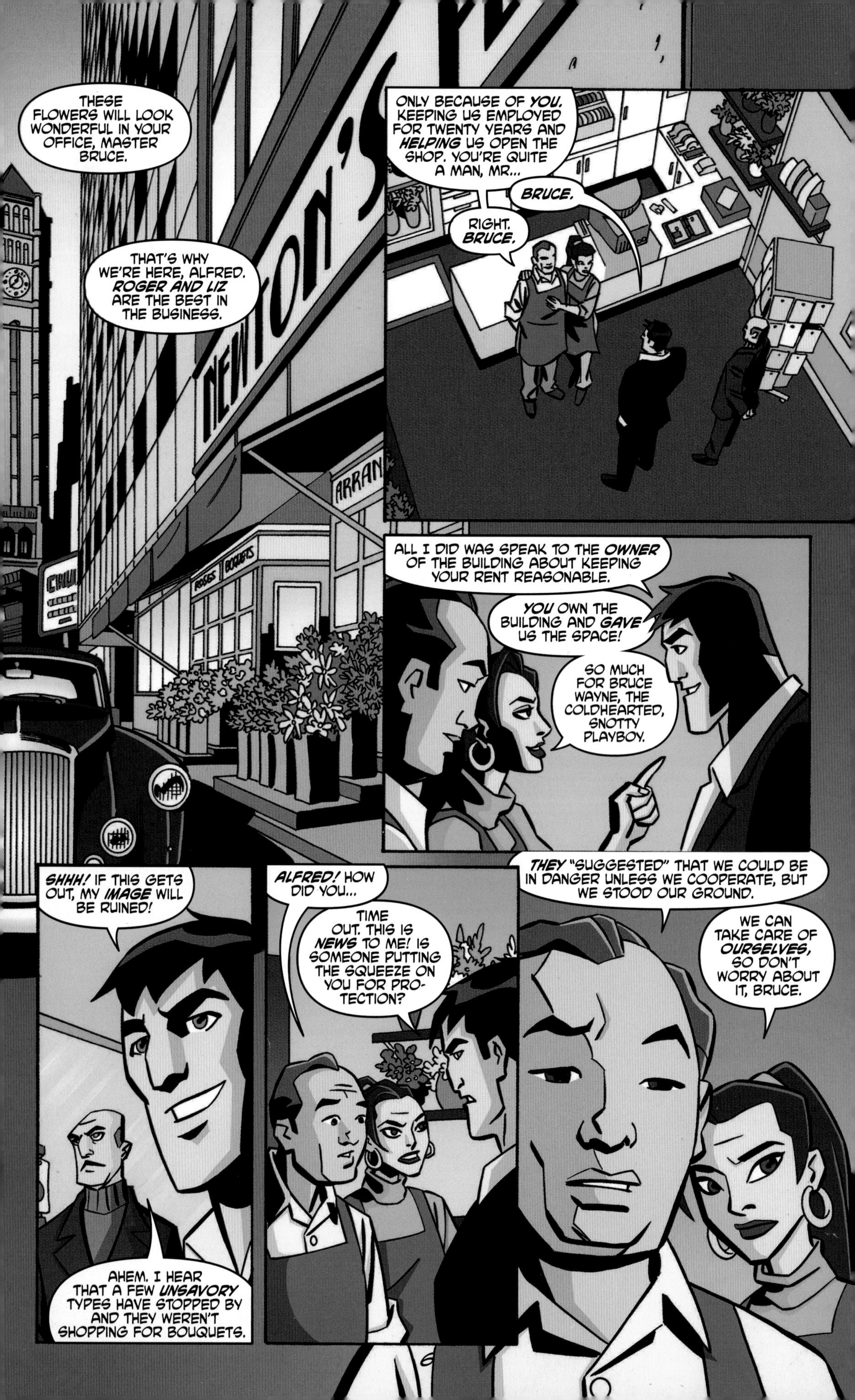
THESE FLOWERS WILL LOOK WONDERFUL IN YOUR OFFICE, MASTER BRUCE.
THAT'S WHY WE'RE HERE, ALFRED. ROGER AND LIZ ARE THE BEST IN THE BUSINESS.
NEWTON'S
ARRAN
ROSES
BOUQUETS
ONLY BECAUSE OF YOU, KEEPING US EMPLOYED FOR TWENTY YEARS AND HELPING US OPEN THE SHOP. YOU'RE QUITE A MAN, MR...
BRUCE.
RIGHT. BRUCE.
ALL I DID WAS SPEAK TO THE OWNER OF THE BUILDING ABOUT KEEPING YOUR RENT REASONABLE.
YOU OWN THE BUILDING AND GAVE US THE SPACE!
SO MUCH FOR BRUCE WAYNE, THE COLDHEARTED, SNOTTY PLAYBOY.
SHHH! IF THIS GETS OUT, MY IMAGE WILL BE RUINED!
AHEM. I HEAR THAT A FEW UNSAVORY TYPES HAVE STOPPED BY AND THEY WEREN'T SHOPPING FOR BOUQUETS.
ALFRED! HOW DID YOU...
TIME OUT. THIS IS NEWS TO ME! IS SOMEONE PUTTING THE SQUEEZE ON YOU FOR PRO-TECTION?
THEY "SUGGESTED" THAT WE COULD BE IN DANGER UNLESS WE COOPERATE, BUT WE STOOD OUR GROUND.
WE CAN TAKE CARE OF OURSELVES, SO DON'T WORRY ABOUT IT, BRUCE.

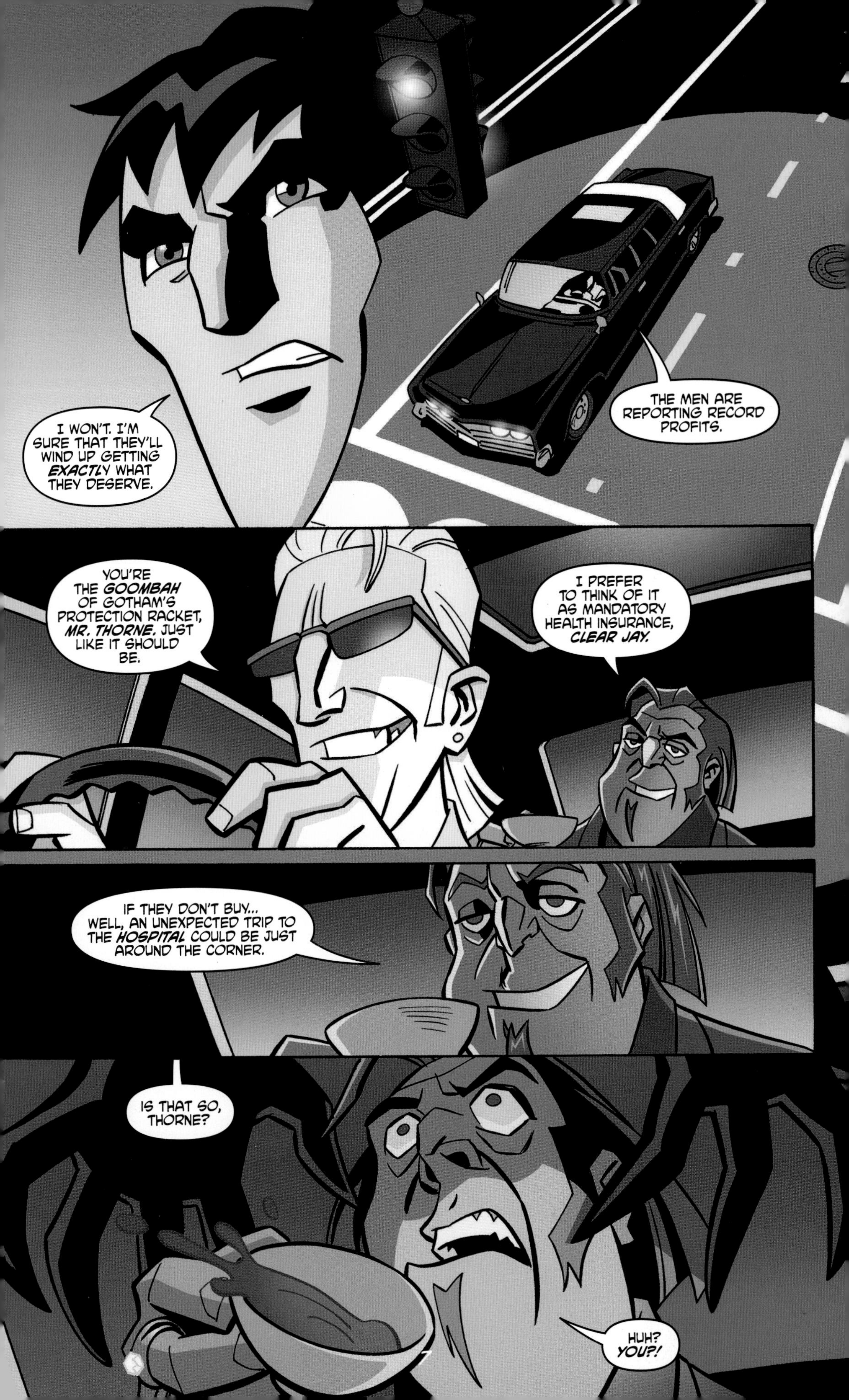
THE MEN ARE REPORTING RECORD PROFITS.
I WON'T. I'M SURE THAT THEY'LL WIND UP GETTING EXACTLY WHAT THEY DESERVE.
YOU'RE THE GOOMBAH OF GOTHAM'S PROTECTION RACKET, MR. THORNE. JUST LIKE IT SHOULD BE.
I PREFER TO THINK OF IT AS MANDATORY HEALTH INSURANCE, CLEAR JAY.
IF THEY DON'T BUY... WELL, AN UNEXPECTED TRIP TO THE HOSPITAL COULD BE JUST AROUND THE CORNER.
IS THAT SO, THORNE?
HUH? YOU?!

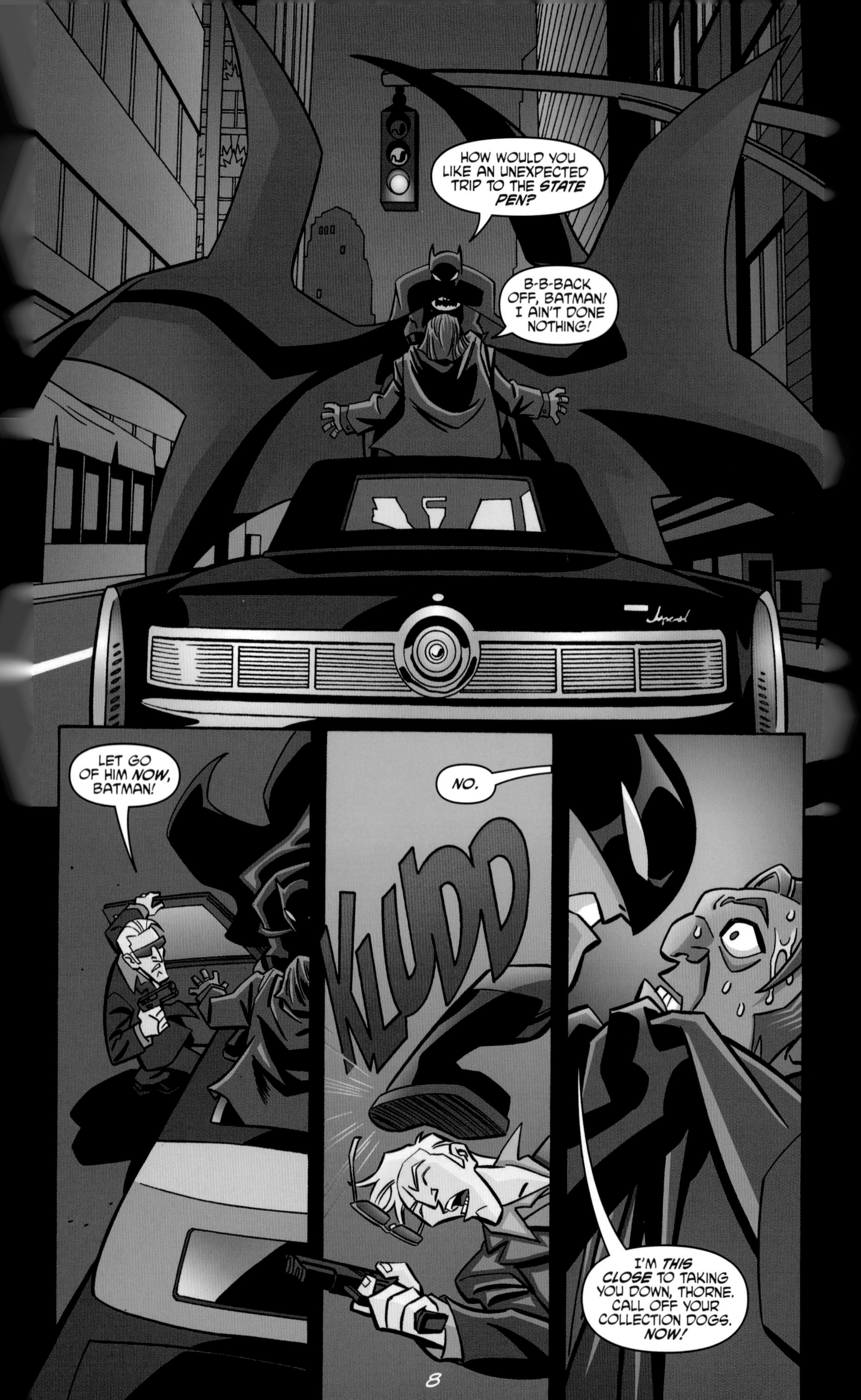
HOW WOULD YOU LIKE AN UNEXPECTED TRIP TO THE STATE PEN?
B-B-BACK OFF, BATMAN! I AIN'T DONE NOTHING!
LET GO OF HIM NOW, BATMAN!
NO.
KLUDD
I'M THIS CLOSE TO TAKING YOU DOWN, THORNE. CALL OFF YOUR COLLECTION DOGS. NOW!

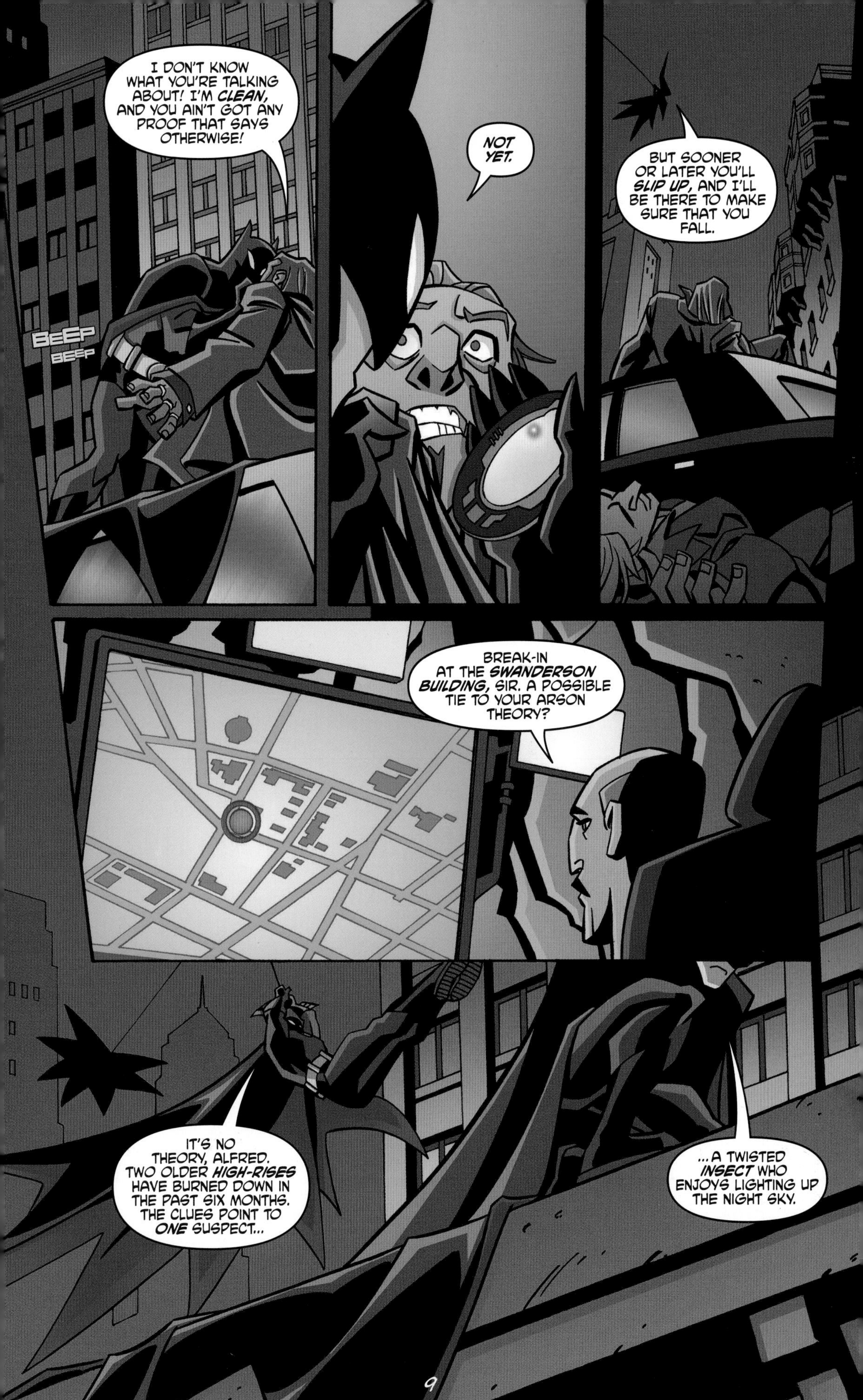
I DON'T KNOW WHAT YOU'RE TALKING ABOUT! I'M *CLEAN*, AND YOU AIN'T GOT ANY PROOF THAT SAYS OTHERWISE!
BEEP BEEP
NOT YET.
BUT SOONER OR LATER YOU'LL *SLIP UP*, AND I'LL BE THERE TO MAKE SURE THAT YOU FALL.
BREAK-IN AT THE *SWANDERSON BUILDING*, SIR. A POSSIBLE TIE TO YOUR ARSON THEORY?
IT'S NO THEORY, ALFRED. TWO OLDER *HIGH-RISES* HAVE BURNED DOWN IN THE PAST SIX MONTHS. THE CLUES POINT TO *ONE* SUSPECT...
...A TWISTED *INSECT* WHO ENJOYS LIGHTING UP THE NIGHT SKY.

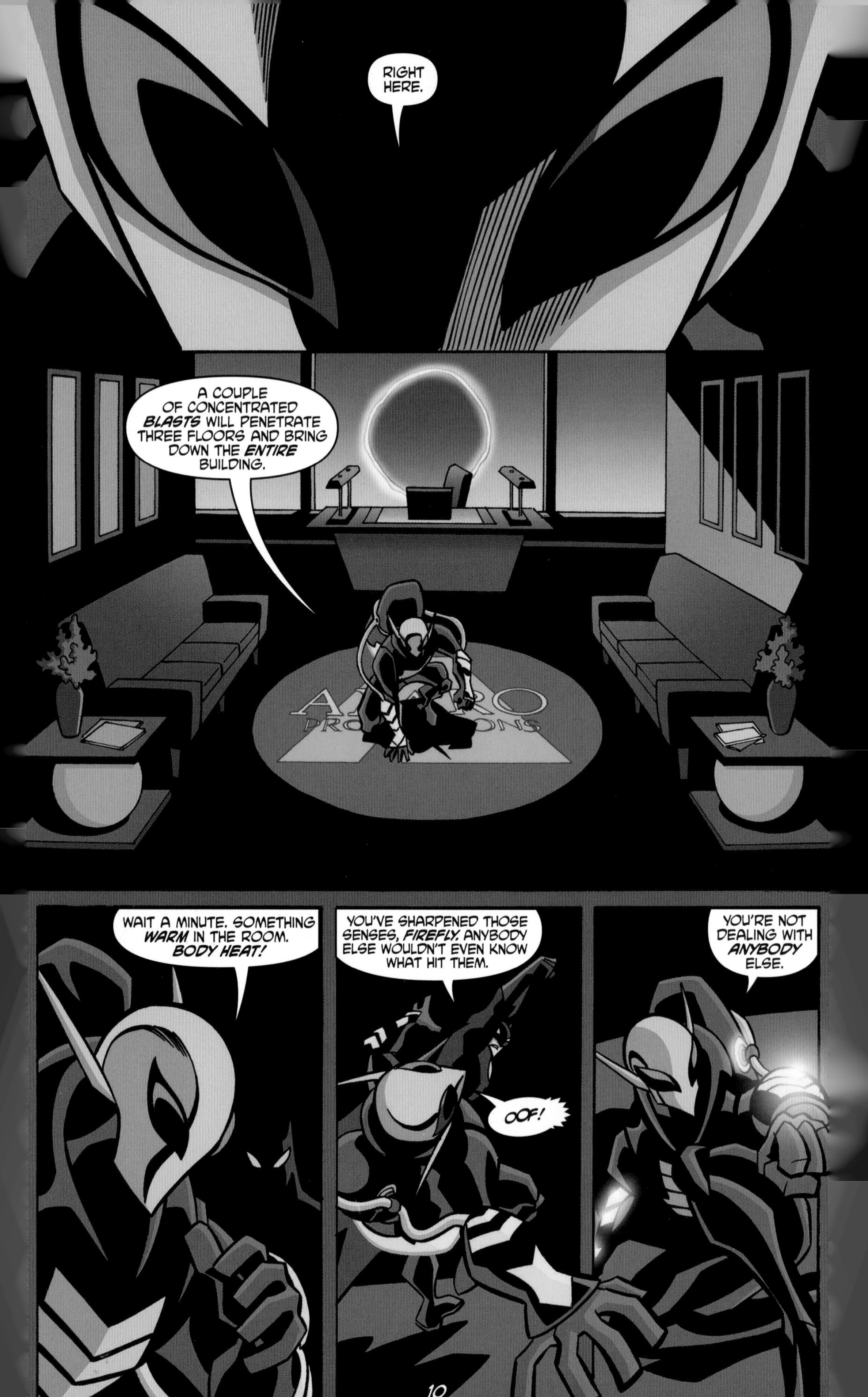
RIGHT HERE.
A COUPLE OF CONCENTRATED BLASTS WILL PENETRATE THREE FLOORS AND BRING DOWN THE ENTIRE BUILDING.
WAIT A MINUTE. SOMETHING WARM IN THE ROOM. BODY HEAT!
YOU'VE SHARPENED THOSE SENSES, FIREFLY. ANYBODY ELSE WOULDN'T EVEN KNOW WHAT HIT THEM.
OOF!
YOU'RE NOT DEALING WITH ANYBODY ELSE.

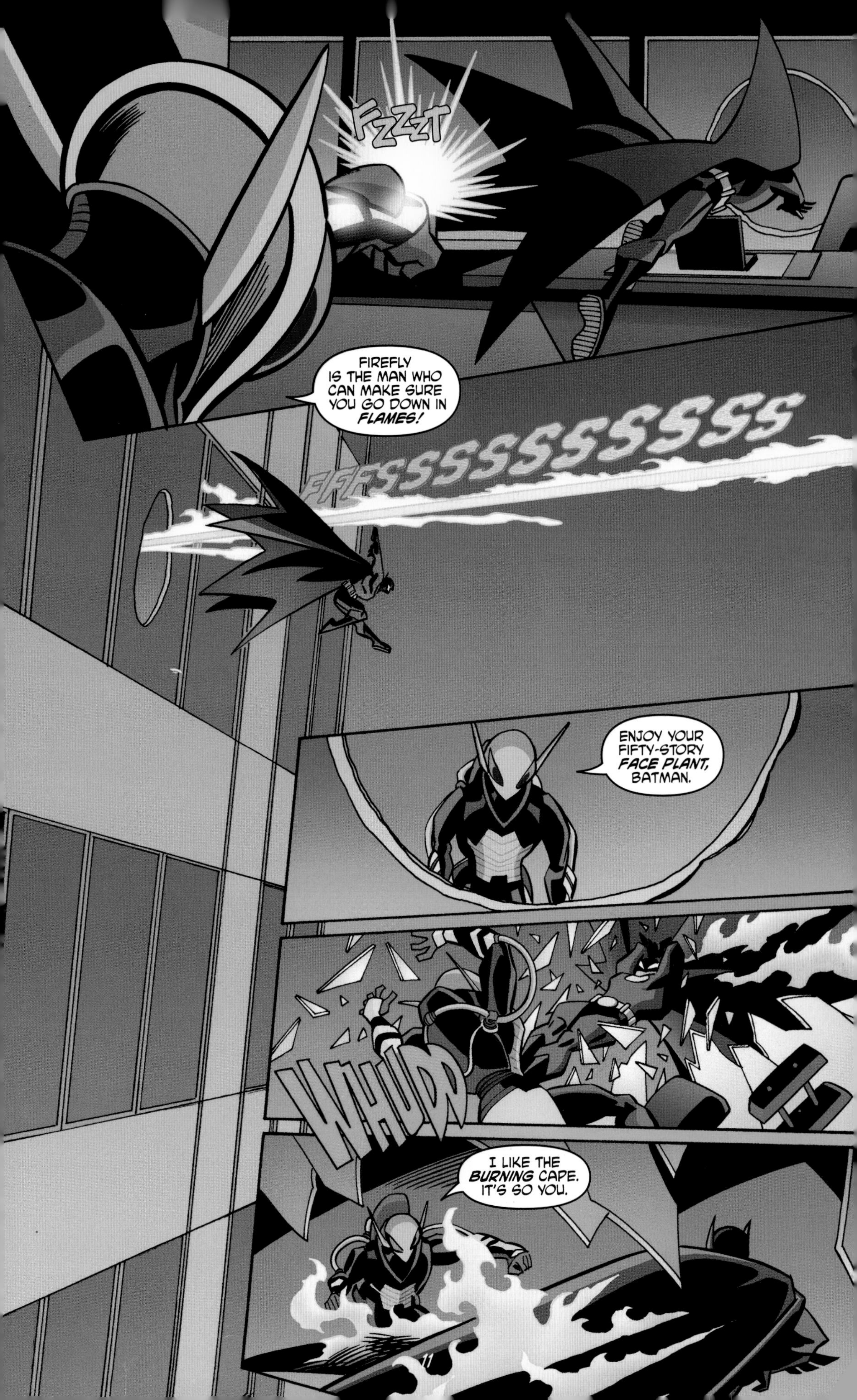
FZZZT
FIREFLY IS THE MAN WHO CAN MAKE SURE YOU GO DOWN IN FLAMES!
FFFSSSSSSSSSSSS
ENJOY YOUR FIFTY-STORY FACE PLANT, BATMAN.
WHUDD
I LIKE THE BURNING CAPE. IT'S SO YOU.

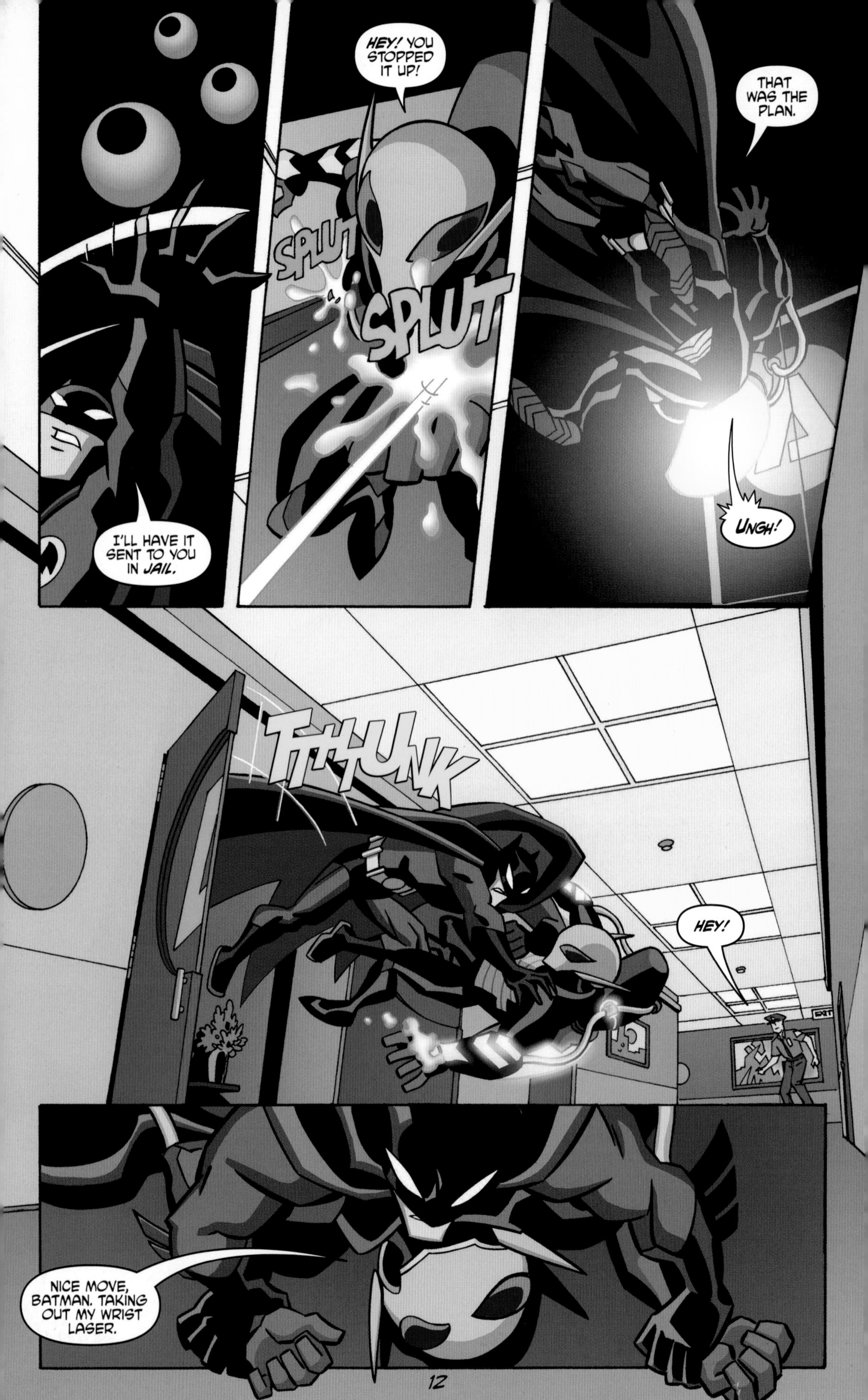
I'LL HAVE IT SENT TO YOU IN JAIL.
SPLUT
SPLUT
HEY! YOU STOPPED IT UP!
THAT WAS THE PLAN.
UNGH!
THHUNK
HEY!
NICE MOVE, BATMAN. TAKING OUT MY WRIST LASER.

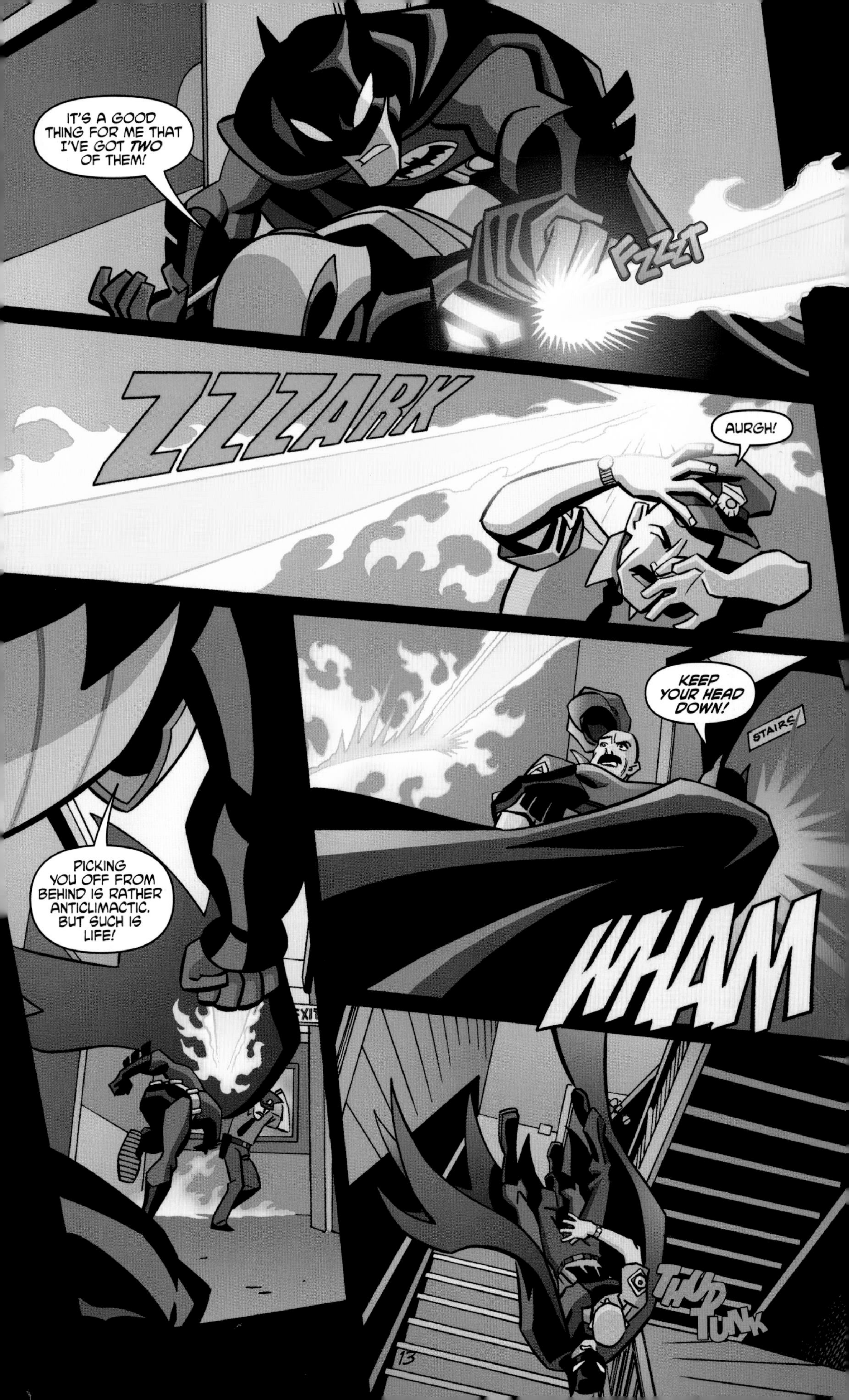
IT'S A GOOD THING FOR ME THAT I'VE GOT TWO OF THEM!
FZZZT
ZZZZARK
AURGH!
KEEP YOUR HEAD DOWN!
STAIRS
PICKING YOU OFF FROM BEHIND IS RATHER ANTICLIMACTIC. BUT SUCH IS LIFE!
WHAM
EXIT
THUD
TUNK

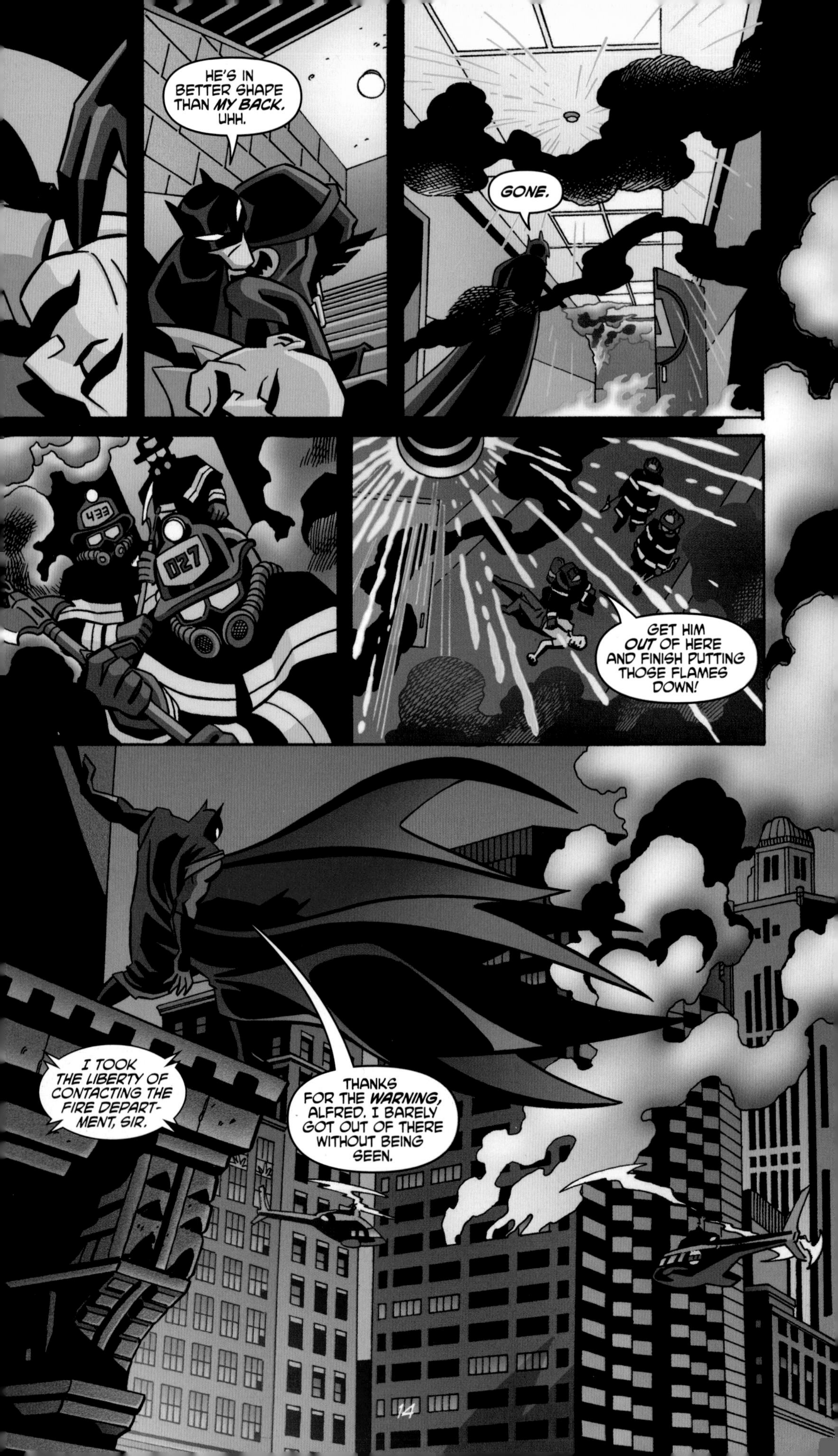
HE'S IN BETTER SHAPE THAN MY BACK. UHH.
GONE.
433
027
GET HIM OUT OF HERE AND FINISH PUTTING THOSE FLAMES DOWN!
I TOOK THE LIBERTY OF CONTACTING THE FIRE DEPARTMENT, SIR.
THANKS FOR THE WARNING, ALFRED. I BARELY GOT OUT OF THERE WITHOUT BEING SEEN.

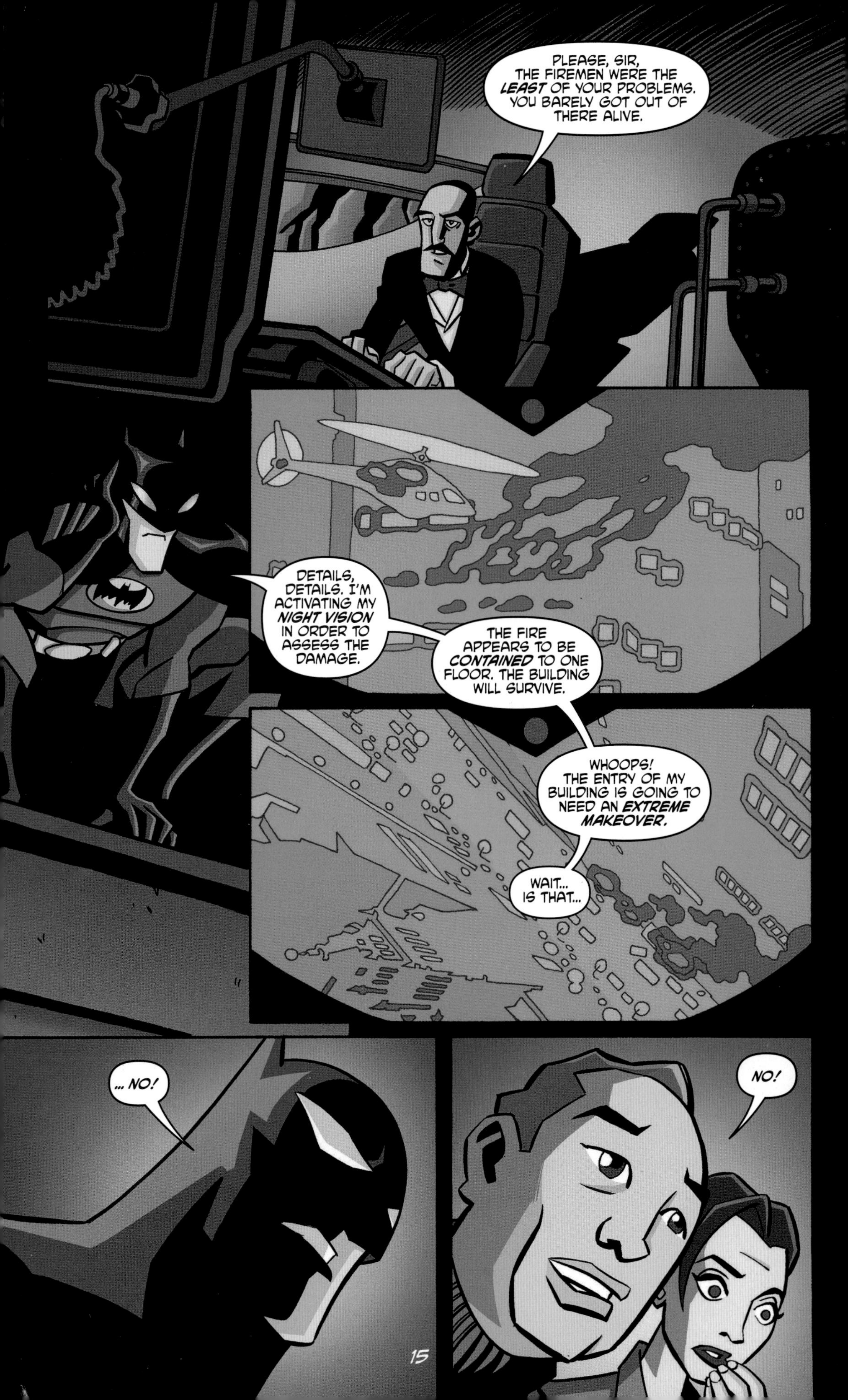
PLEASE, SIR, THE FIREMEN WERE THE LEAST OF YOUR PROBLEMS. YOU BARELY GOT OUT OF THERE ALIVE.
DETAILS, DETAILS. I'M ACTIVATING MY NIGHT VISION IN ORDER TO ASSESS THE DAMAGE.
THE FIRE APPEARS TO BE CONTAINED TO ONE FLOOR. THE BUILDING WILL SURVIVE.
WHOOPS! THE ENTRY OF MY BUILDING IS GOING TO NEED AN EXTREME MAKEOVER.
WAIT... IS THAT...
... NO!
NO!

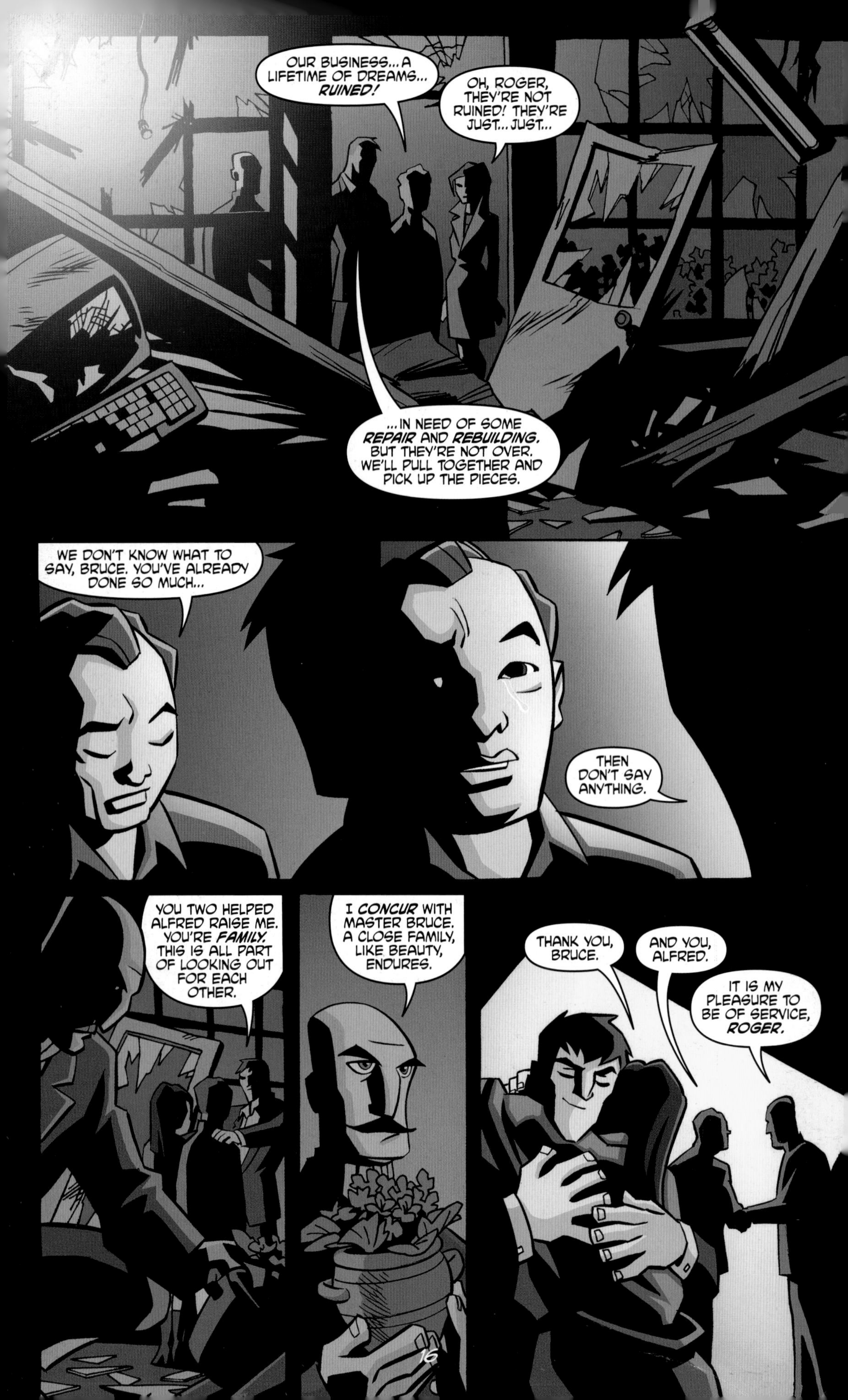
OUR BUSINESS... A LIFETIME OF DREAMS... RUINED!
OH, ROGER, THEY'RE NOT RUINED! THEY'RE JUST... JUST...
...IN NEED OF SOME REPAIR AND REBUILDING. BUT THEY'RE NOT OVER. WE'LL PULL TOGETHER AND PICK UP THE PIECES.
WE DON'T KNOW WHAT TO SAY, BRUCE. YOU'VE ALREADY DONE SO MUCH...
THEN DON'T SAY ANYTHING.
YOU TWO HELPED ALFRED RAISE ME. YOU'RE FAMILY. THIS IS ALL PART OF LOOKING OUT FOR EACH OTHER.
I CONCUR WITH MASTER BRUCE. A CLOSE FAMILY, LIKE BEAUTY, ENDURES.
THANK YOU, BRUCE.
AND YOU, ALFRED.
IT IS MY PLEASURE TO BE OF SERVICE, ROGER.

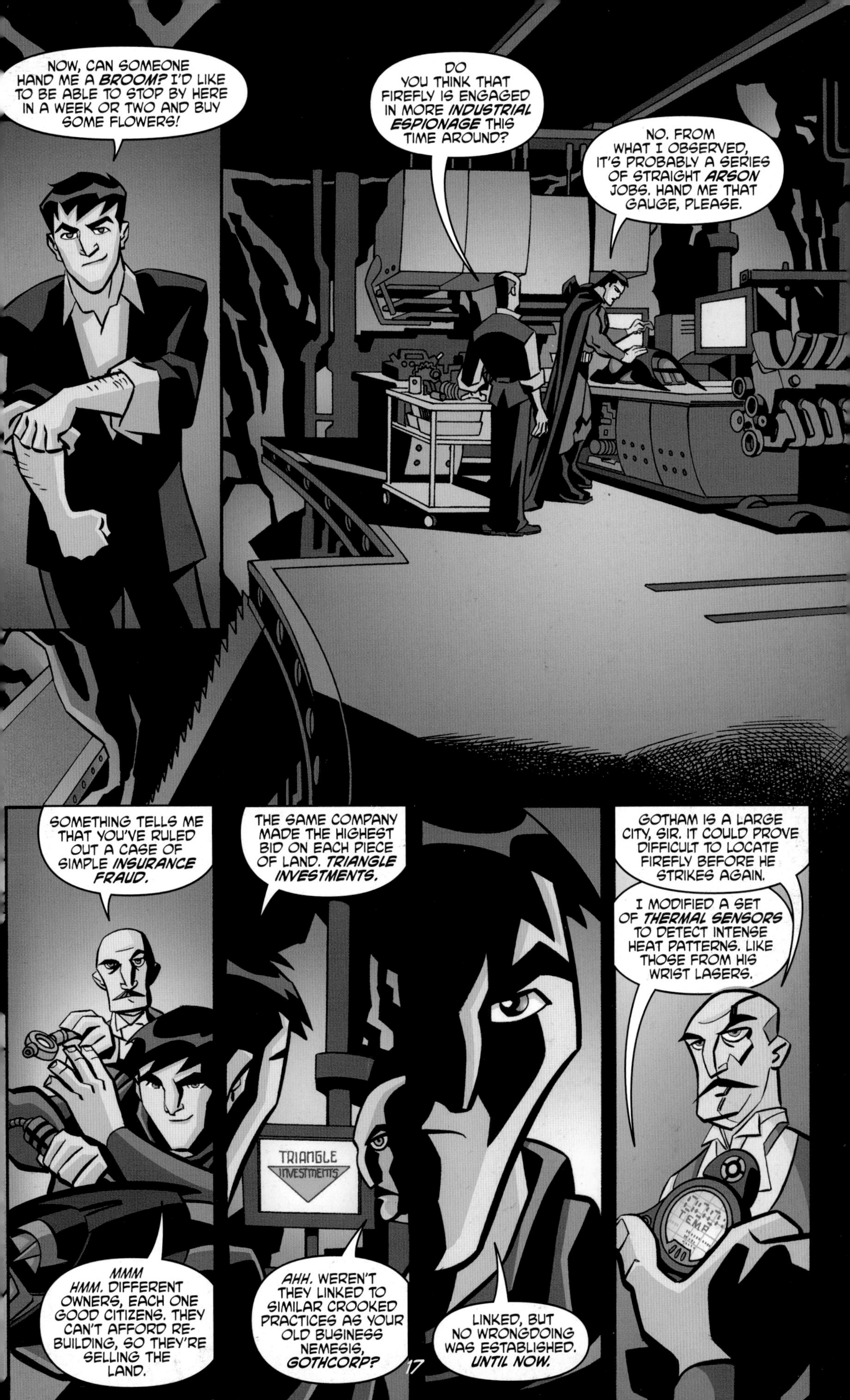
NOW, CAN SOMEONE HAND ME A BROOM? I'D LIKE TO BE ABLE TO STOP BY HERE IN A WEEK OR TWO AND BUY SOME FLOWERS!
DO YOU THINK THAT FIREFLY IS ENGAGED IN MORE INDUSTRIAL ESPIONAGE THIS TIME AROUND?
NO. FROM WHAT I OBSERVED, IT'S PROBABLY A SERIES OF STRAIGHT ARSON JOBS. HAND ME THAT GAUGE, PLEASE.
SOMETHING TELLS ME THAT YOU'VE RULED OUT A CASE OF SIMPLE INSURANCE FRAUD.
MMM HMM. DIFFERENT OWNERS, EACH ONE GOOD CITIZENS. THEY CAN'T AFFORD RE-BUILDING, SO THEY'RE SELLING THE LAND.
THE SAME COMPANY MADE THE HIGHEST BID ON EACH PIECE OF LAND. TRIANGLE INVESTMENTS.
TRIANGLE INVESTMENTS
AHH. WEREN'T THEY LINKED TO SIMILAR CROOKED PRACTICES AS YOUR OLD BUSINESS NEMESIS, GOTHCORP?
LINKED, BUT NO WRONGDOING WAS ESTABLISHED. UNTIL NOW.
GOTHAM IS A LARGE CITY, SIR. IT COULD PROVE DIFFICULT TO LOCATE FIREFLY BEFORE HE STRIKES AGAIN.
I MODIFIED A SET OF THERMAL SENSORS TO DETECT INTENSE HEAT PATTERNS. LIKE THOSE FROM HIS WRIST LASERS.
TEMP

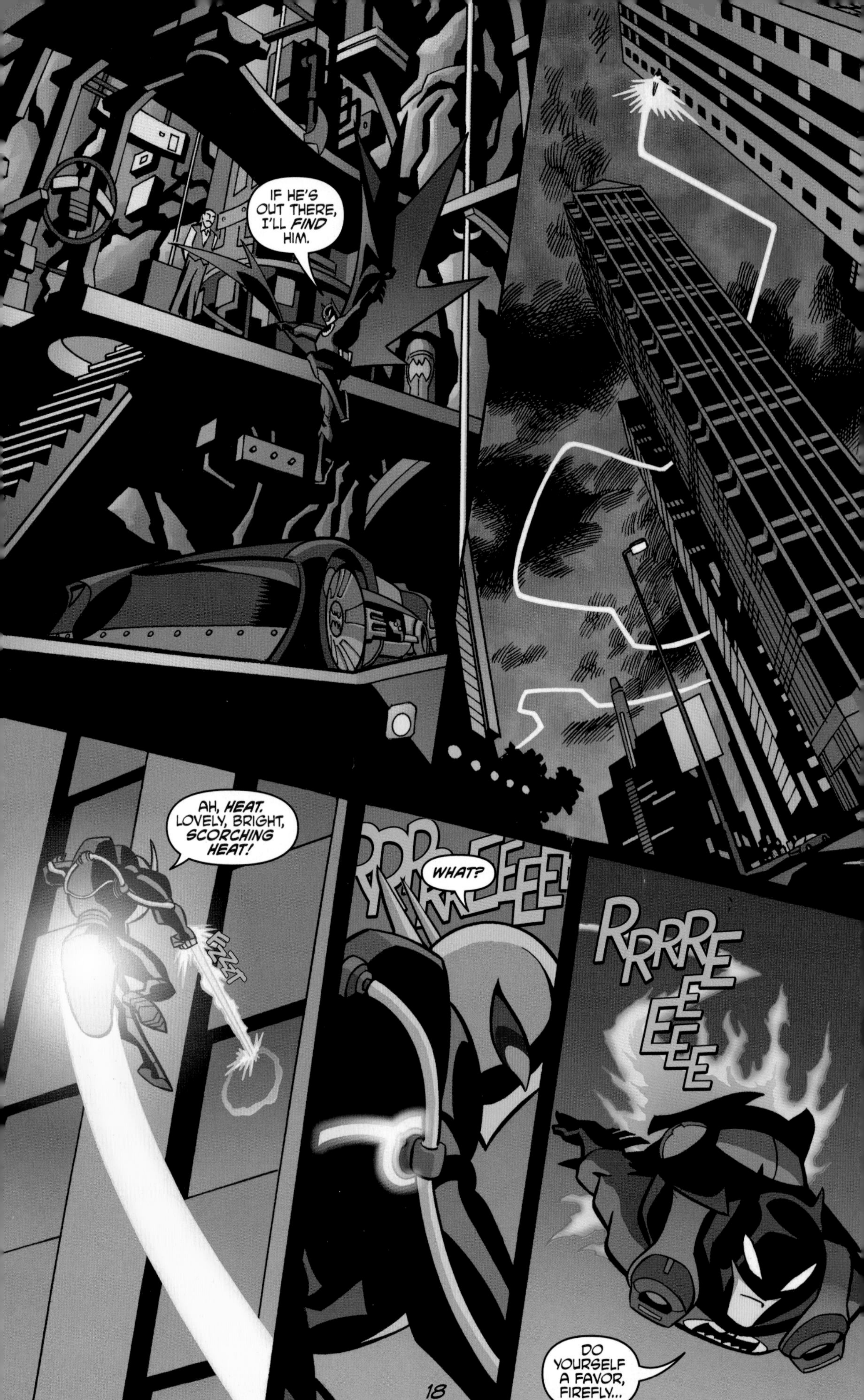
IF HE'S OUT THERE, I'LL *FIND* HIM.
AH, *HEAT*. LOVELY, BRIGHT, *SCORCHING HEAT!*
FZZT
RRRREEEEEE
WHAT?
RRRREEEEE
DO YOURSELF A FAVOR, FIREFLY...

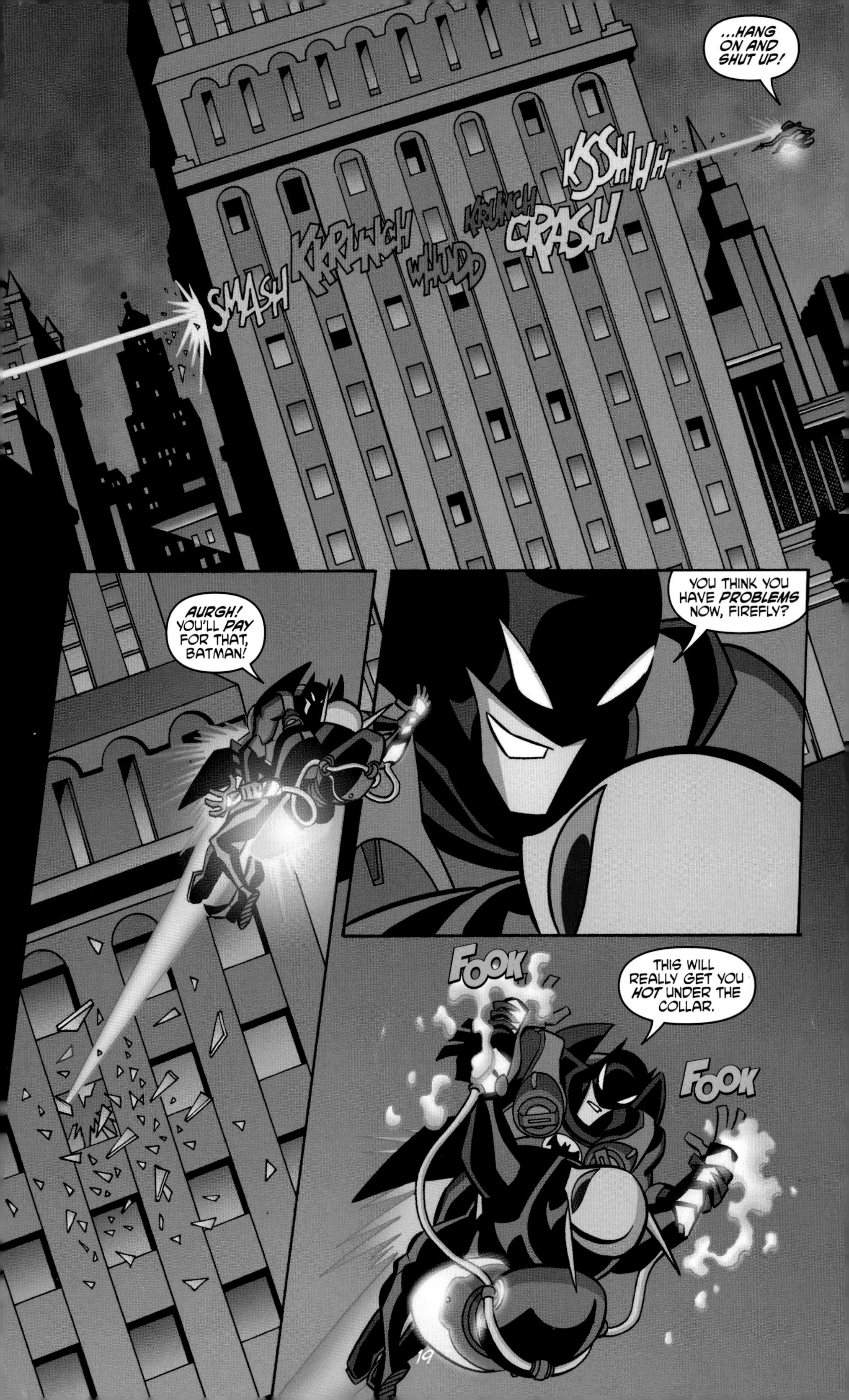
...HANG ON AND SHUT UP!
SMASH
KKRUNCH
WHUDD
KRUNCH
CRASH
KSSHHH
AURGH! YOU'LL PAY FOR THAT, BATMAN!
YOU THINK YOU HAVE PROBLEMS NOW, FIREFLY?
FOOK
FOOK
THIS WILL REALLY GET YOU HOT UNDER THE COLLAR.

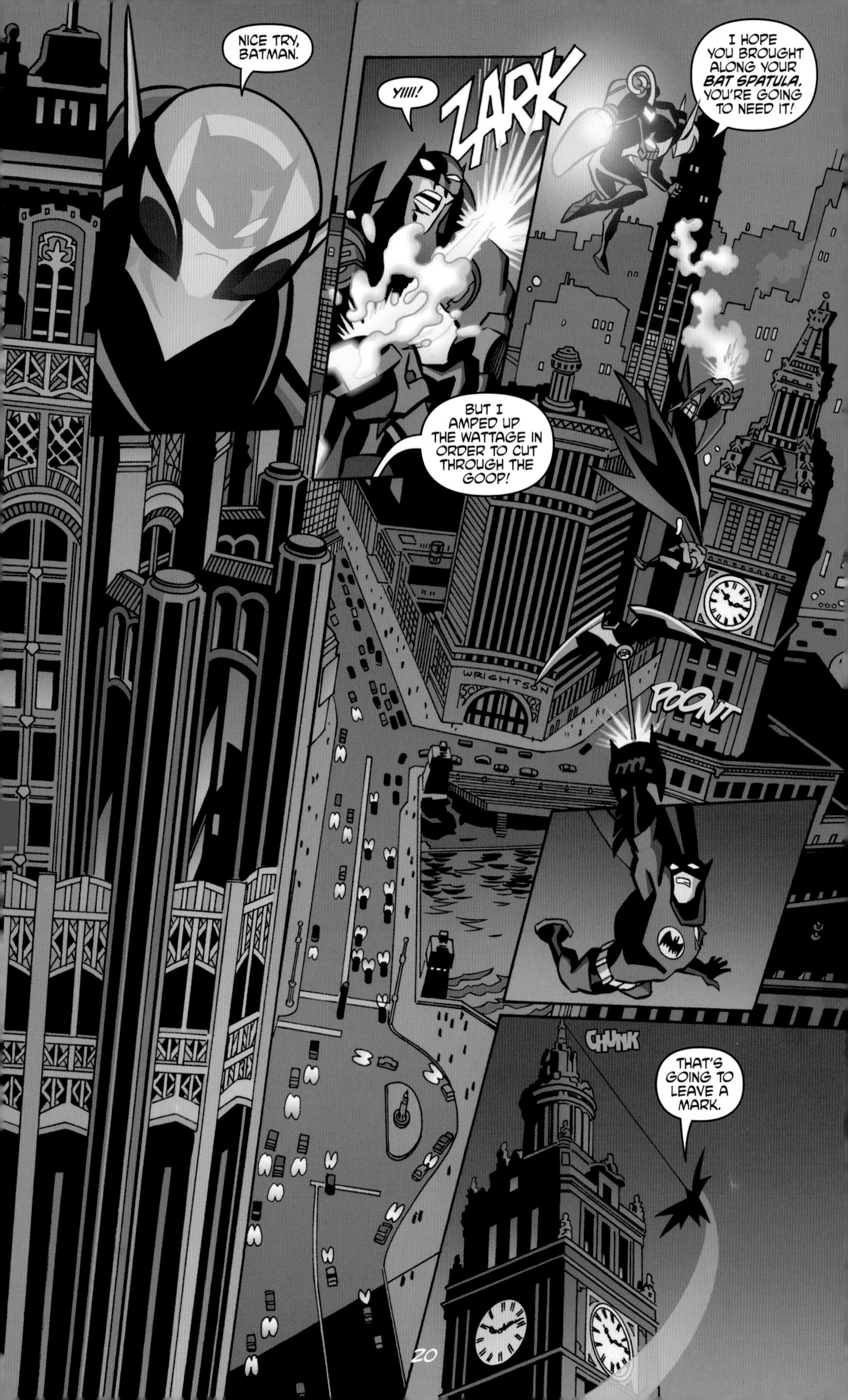
NICE TRY, BATMAN.
YIIII!
ZARK
I HOPE YOU BROUGHT ALONG YOUR BAT SPATULA. YOU'RE GOING TO NEED IT!
BUT I AMPED UP THE WATTAGE IN ORDER TO CUT THROUGH THE GOOP!
WRIGHTSON
POONT
CHUNK
THAT'S GOING TO LEAVE A MARK.

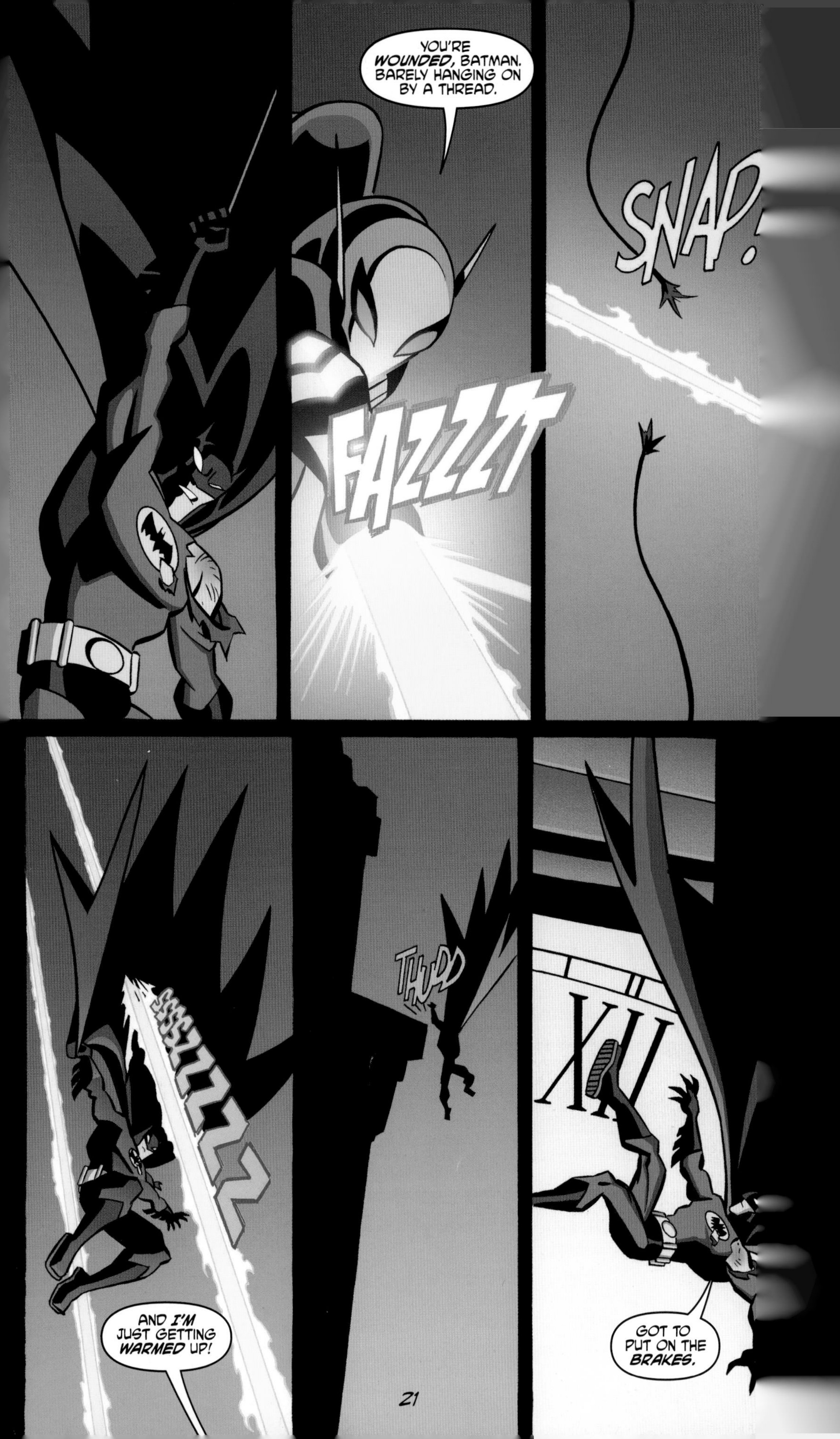
YOU'RE WOUNDED, BATMAN. BARELY HANGING ON BY A THREAD.
FAZZZT
SNAP!
SSSZZZZZ
AND I'M JUST GETTING WARMED UP!
THUDD
GOT TO PUT ON THE BRAKES.

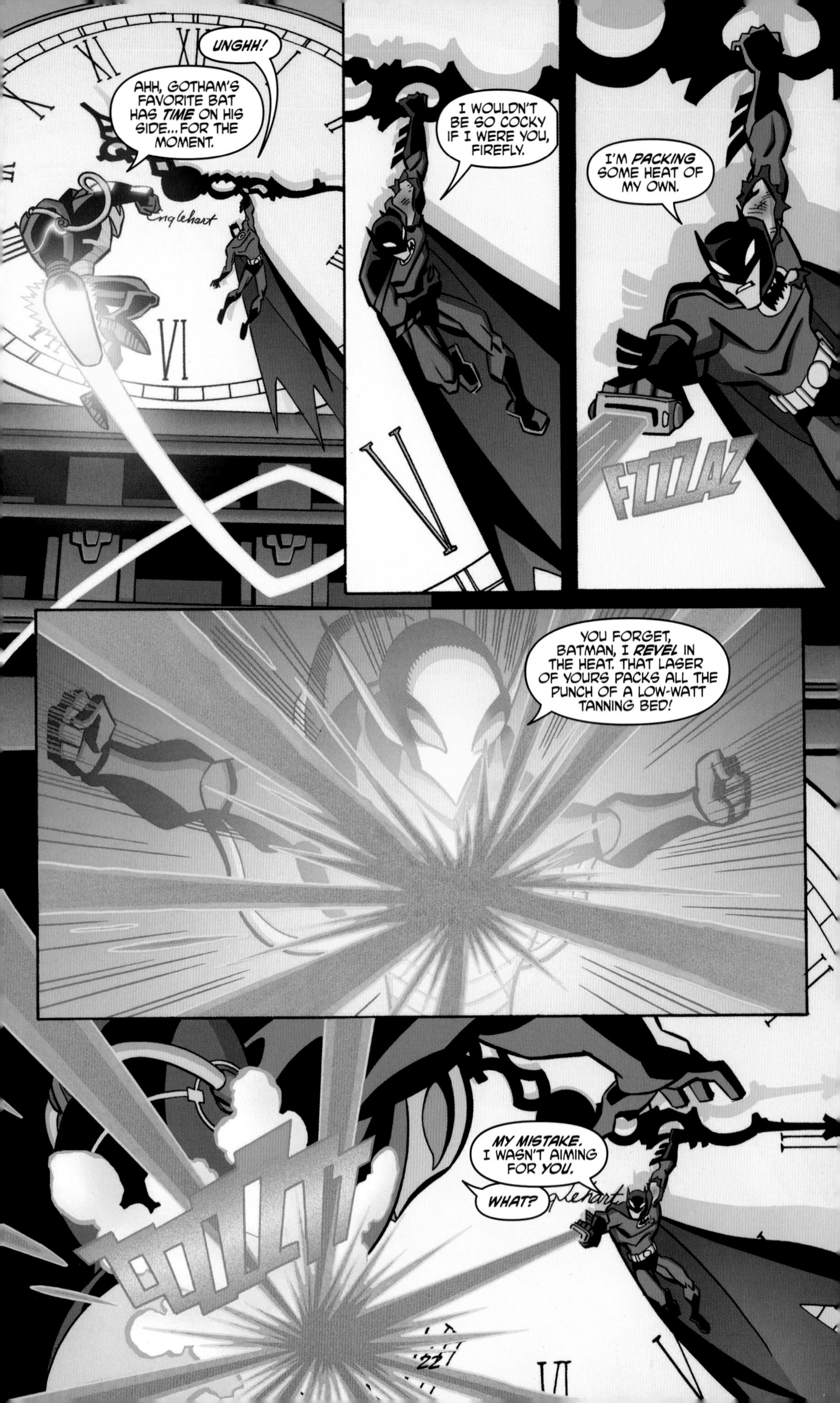
UNGHH!
AHH, GOTHAM'S FAVORITE BAT HAS *TIME* ON HIS SIDE... FOR THE MOMENT.
I WOULDN'T BE SO COCKY IF I WERE YOU, FIREFLY.
I'M *PACKING* SOME HEAT OF MY OWN.
YOU FORGET, BATMAN, I *REVEL* IN THE HEAT. THAT LASER OF YOURS PACKS ALL THE PUNCH OF A LOW-WATT TANNING BED!
MY MISTAKE. I WASN'T AIMING FOR *YOU.*
WHAT?

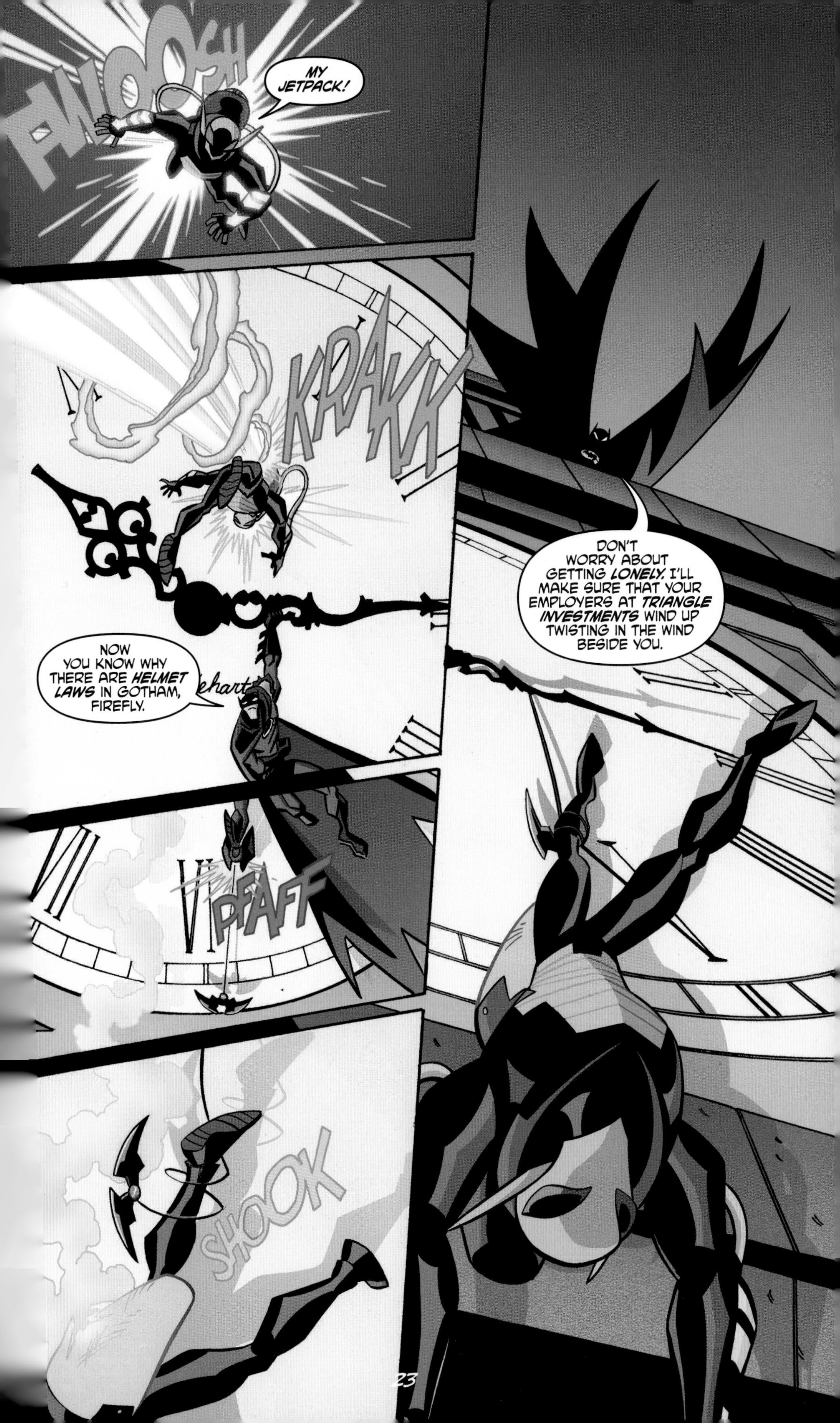
FWOOSH
MY JETPACK!
KRAKK
NOW YOU KNOW WHY THERE ARE HELMET LAWS IN GOTHAM, FIREFLY.
PFAFF
SHOOK
DON'T WORRY ABOUT GETTING LONELY. I'LL MAKE SURE THAT YOUR EMPLOYERS AT TRIANGLE INVESTMENTS WIND UP TWISTING IN THE WIND BESIDE YOU.

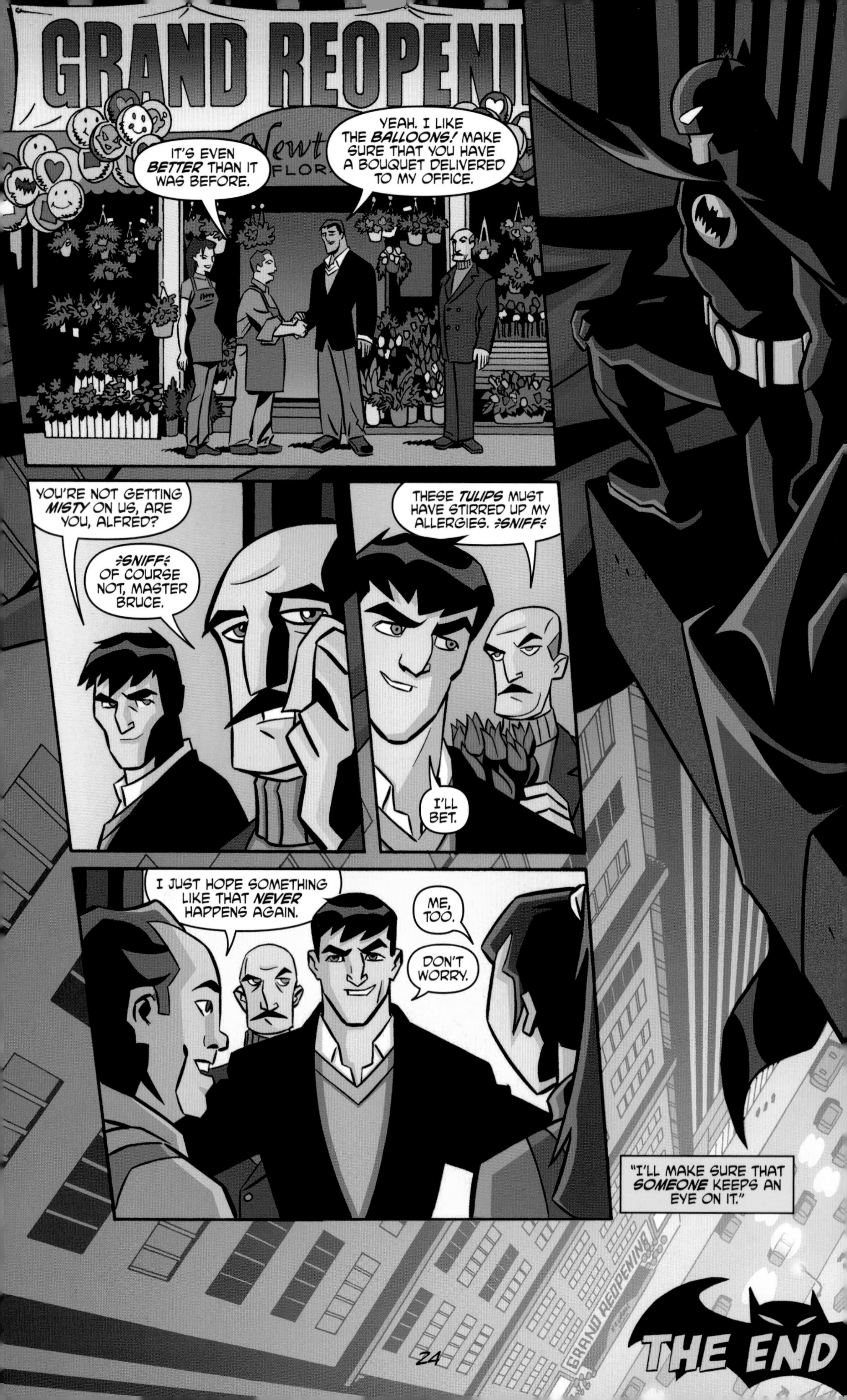
GRAND REOPENI
IT'S EVEN BETTER THAN IT WAS BEFORE.
YEAH. I LIKE THE BALLOONS! MAKE SURE THAT YOU HAVE A BOUQUET DELIVERED TO MY OFFICE.
YOU'RE NOT GETTING MISTY ON US, ARE YOU, ALFRED?
SNIFF OF COURSE NOT, MASTER BRUCE.
THESE TULIPS MUST HAVE STIRRED UP MY ALLERGIES. SNIFF
I'LL BET.
I JUST HOPE SOMETHING LIKE THAT NEVER HAPPENS AGAIN.
ME, TOO.
DON'T WORRY.
"I'LL MAKE SURE THAT SOMEONE KEEPS AN EYE ON IT."
GRAND REOPENING
THE END

CREATORS

BILL MATHENY WRITER
Along with comics like THE BATMAN STRIKES, Bill Matheny has written for TV series including KRYPTO THE SUPERDOG, WHERE'S WALDO, A PUP NAMED SCOOBY-DOO, and many others.

CHRISTOPHER JONES PENCILLER
Christopher Jones is an artist that has worked for DC Comics, Image, Malibu, Caliber, and Sundragon Comics.

TERRY BEATTY INKER
Terry Beatty has inked THE BATMAN STRIKES! and BATMAN: THE BRAVE AND THE BOLD as well as several other DC Comics graphic novels.

GLOSSARY

anticlimactic (an-tye-kly-MAK-tik)--if something is anticlimactic, then it seems far less important or dramatic than expected

arson (AR-son)--the crime of setting fire to something

assess (uh-SESS)--to evaluate or take stock of something

concur (KUHN-ker)--if you concur, you agree

endures (en-DYOORZ)--survives or lasts through a process

espionage (ESS-pee-oh-nahj)--the activity of spying

fraud (FROD)--the crime of using dishonest methods to take something valuable from someone

mandatory (MAN-duh-tor-ee)--required by law or rules

revel (REV-uhl)--if you revel in something, you take great satisfaction from it

unsavory (un-SAVE-or-ee)--unpleasant in taste or smell, or disagreeable

VISUAL QUESTIONS & PROMPTS

1. Why do you think the comic book's creators chose to have Batman's Batarang overlap the panel's border here?

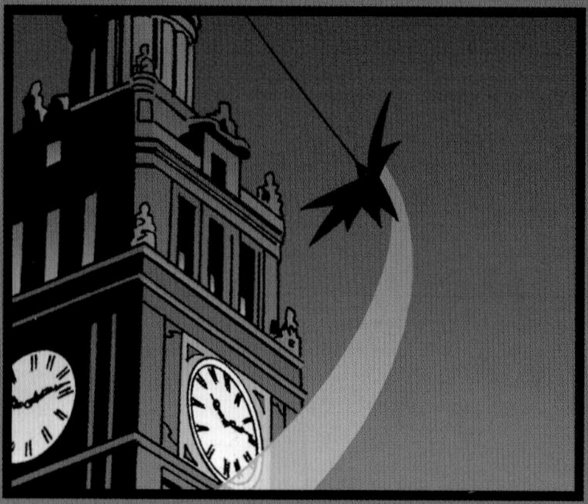

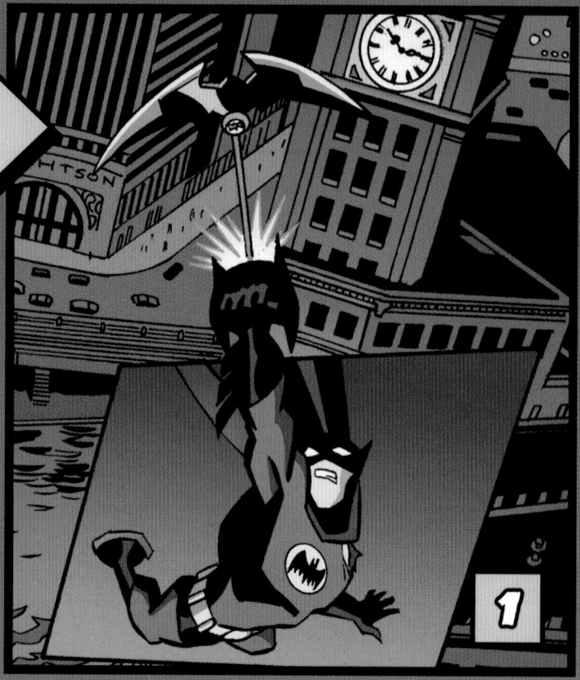
1

2. Why are there sound effects, or SFX, in this panel? Describe the various things that happen in this single panel.

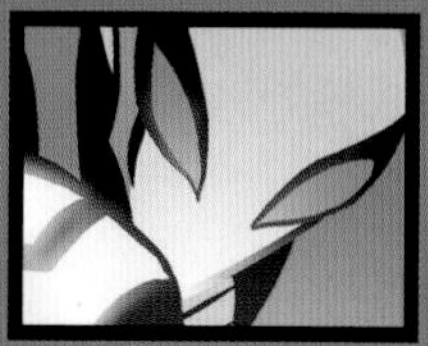

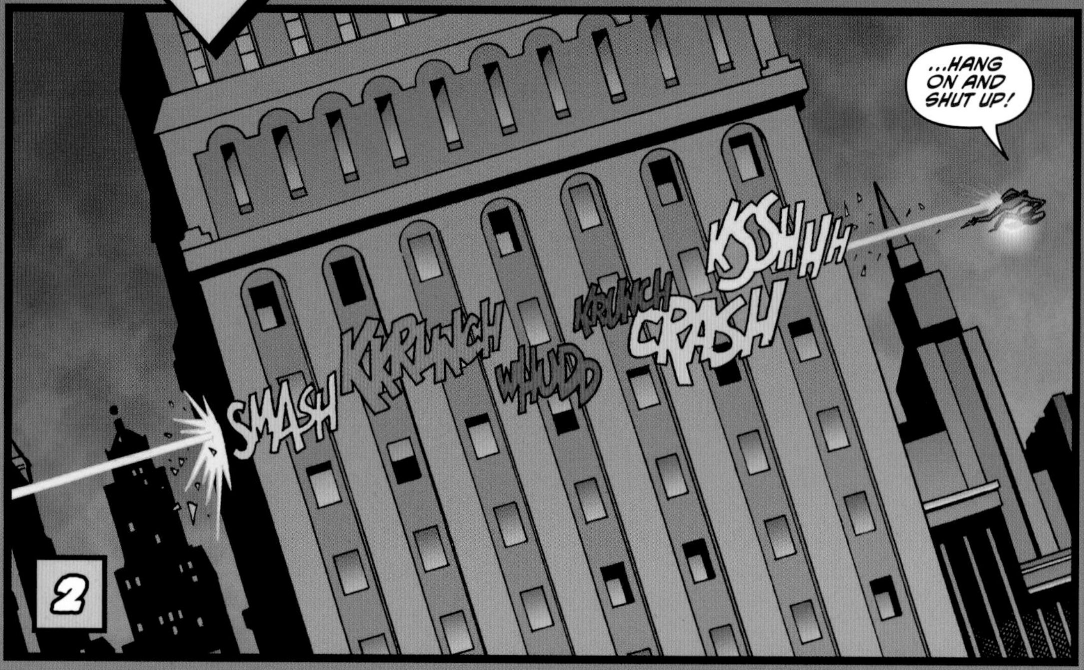
...HANG ON AND SHUT UP!
SMASH
KKRUNCH
WHUDD
KRUNCH
CRASH
KSSHHHH
2

3. Batman's night vision allows him to see in the dark. In what ways does this give him an advantage against criminals?

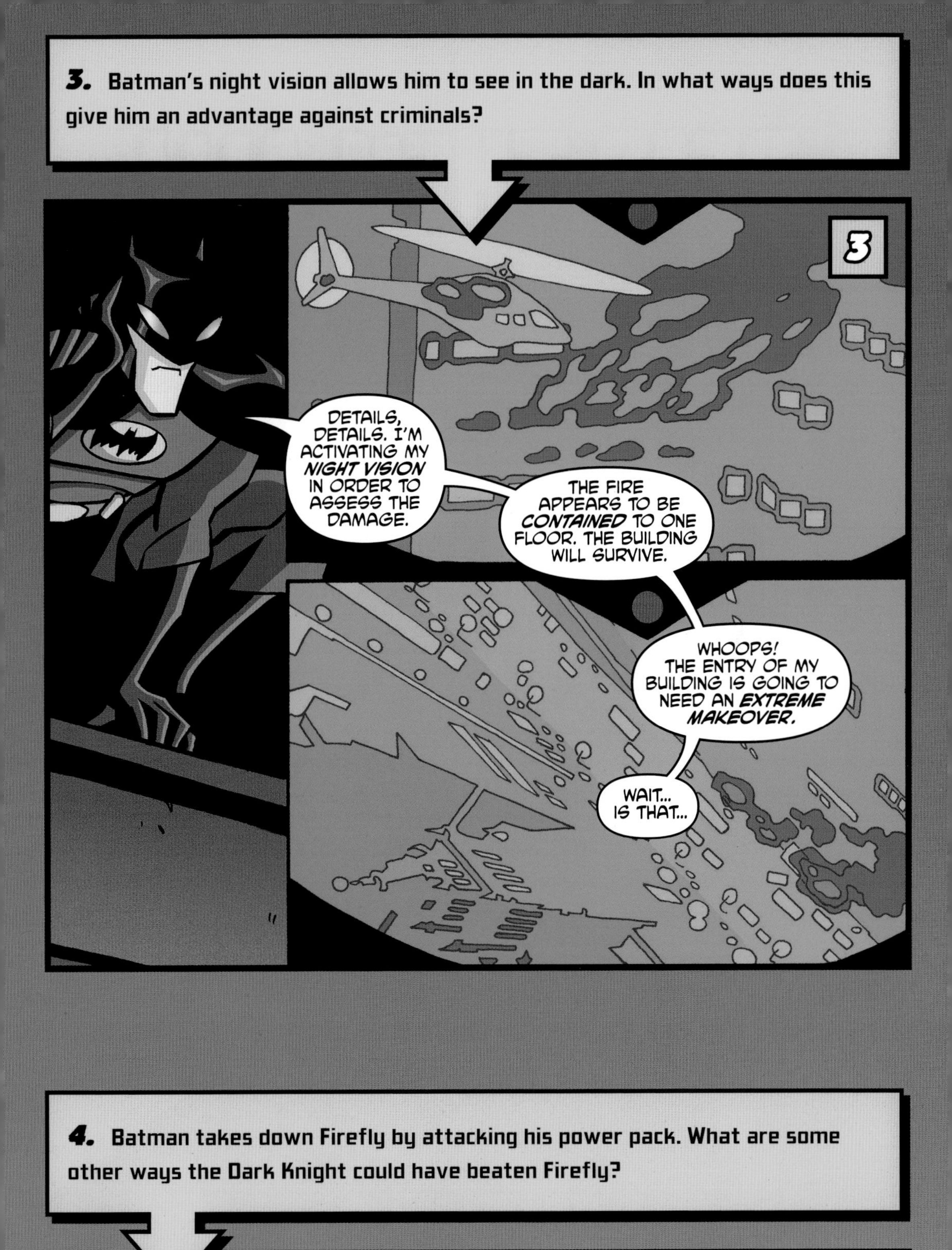
3
DETAILS, DETAILS. I'M ACTIVATING MY *NIGHT VISION* IN ORDER TO ASSESS THE DAMAGE.
THE FIRE APPEARS TO BE *CONTAINED* TO ONE FLOOR. THE BUILDING WILL SURVIVE.
WHOOPS! THE ENTRY OF MY BUILDING IS GOING TO NEED AN *EXTREME MAKEOVER.*
WAIT... IS THAT...

4. Batman takes down Firefly by attacking his power pack. What are some other ways the Dark Knight could have beaten Firefly?

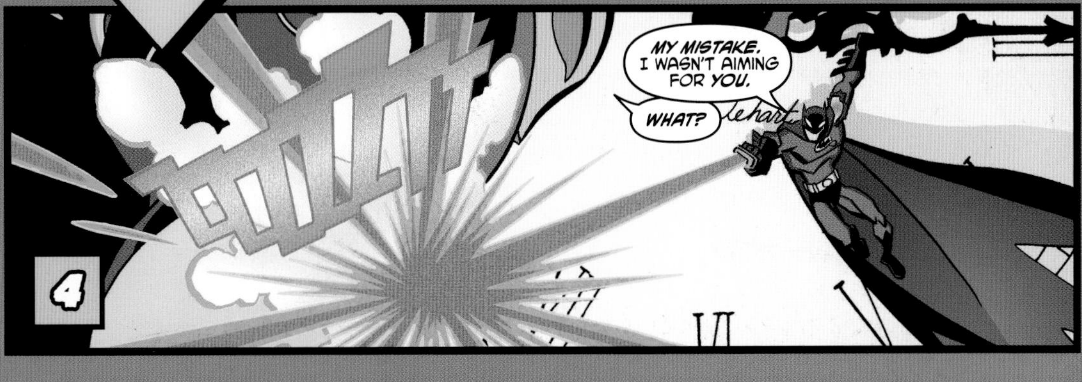
MY MISTAKE. I WASN'T AIMING FOR *YOU.*
WHAT?
4

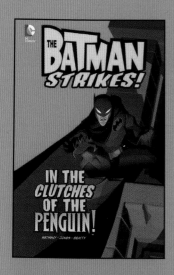

THE BATMAN STRIKES!®

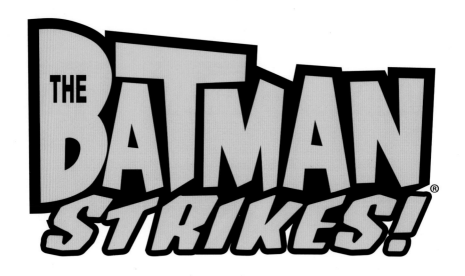